What's what?

What's what?
A Guessing Game

Mary Serfozo

illustrated by
Keiko Narahashi

Margaret K. McElderry Books

For the "distant" cousins: Dana, Sara, Jonathan, and Aaron Serfozo;
Chris, Jay, Sean, and Matthew Cullinan; James and Brian Holle.

—M.S.

For Patrick and Julia and Stanford

—K.N.

Other books by Mary Serfozo and Keiko Narahashi:

Rain Talk

Who Wants One?

Who Said Red?

(Margaret K. McElderry Books)

Margaret K. McElderry Books
An imprint of the Simon & Schuster Children's Publishing Division
1230 Avenue of the Americas
New York, NY 10020

Book design by Ann Bobco
The text of this book was set in Univers Extra Black
The illustrations were rendered in watercolor

Printed in Hong Kong by South China Printing Co. (1988) Ltd.
First Edition
10 9 8 7 6 5 4 3 2

Library of Congress Cataloging-in-Publication Data
Serfozo, Mary.
What's what? / Mary Serfozo; illustrated by Keiko Narahashi.—1st ed.
p. cm.
Summary: Illustrations and rhyming text provide examples of what is soft and hard,
warm and cold, wet and dry, long and short, and light and dark
and describe how a puppy is all these things at once.
ISBN 0–689–80653–1
[1. English language—Synonyms and antonyms—Fiction. 2. Dogs—Fiction.]
I. Narahashi, Keiko, ill. II. Title.
PZ7.S482Wg   1996
[E]—dc20
95–40098
CIP
AC

What's

hard?

A sidewalk is hard
as a rock or a wall.
So look out where you fall!

What's

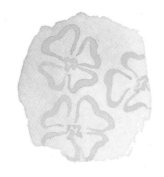

soft?

A lap's nice and soft
like your favorite bear
and the pillow you share.

What's

cold?

Ice cream is cold
as the sea spray that blows.
Wave foam chasing your toes.

What's

warm?

Slippers are warm.
So's a snuggly hug
on the fireside rug.

What's

wet?

**Raindrops are wet,
puddles fun to explore,
boots that drip on the floor.**

What's

dry?

**Paper is dry,
so are flour and chalk,
puffs of dust where you walk.**

What's

long?

Train tracks are long.
And long trains on the track
go away and come back.

What's

short?

Shorts are sure short.
So's a short-legged stool,
or a shortcut to school.

What's

light?

Daytime is light.
All the things bright and clear
that your eyes see from here.

What's

dark?

Nighttime is dark.
So is brown, so is black.
So's a cave—way, way back.

But . . .

what's

soft and hard

and warm and cold

and wet and dry

and

long and **short**

and **light** and **dark**

all at the same **time?**

It's this puppy!

His nails are hard.
His nose is wet and cold.
His ears are   short.

His tail is long.
His hair is dark.
His paws are light.

And he's soft and warm and dry!